Art and Craft
ADVENTURES 1

Mary Carroll • Katie Long

THE O'BRIEN PRESS
PINE FOREST ART

First published 2001 by The O'Brien Press Ltd.
20 Victoria Road, Dublin 6, Ireland
Tel. +353 1 4923333; Fax. +353 1 4922777
e-mail: books@obrien.ie
website: www.obrien.ie
Co-published with Pine Forest Art Centre

ISBN 0-86278-683-5

British Library Cataloguing-in-publication Data
A catalogue reference for this title is available from the British Library

1 2 3 4 5 6 7 8 9 10
01 02 03 04 05 06 07 08

Cover and prelims layout and design: The O'Brien Press Ltd.
Photographs: Dennis Mortell
Colour separations for cover: C&A Print, Ireland
Printed in Italy

CONTENTS

Leaves

Materials

- Leaves
- White paper
- Coloured paper
- Glue
- Coloured crayons
- Pencils

Equipment

- Scissors

Starting Point

Collect lots of differently shaped leaves, especially ones with interesting edges and veins that stick out.

1 Place a leaf under a piece of white paper. Using a crayon on its side, rub over the paper on top of the leaf.

3 Cut the leaves out carefully.

Trouble Shooter
Make sure the leaf stays very still under the paper and doesn't move while rubbing.

2 Take a different colour crayon and blend it into the first one, paying particular attention to the edges.

4 Draw the outline of a tree, with lots of branches, on coloured paper and cut it out.

5 Arrange the tree with its leaves on a coloured background and glue everything in place.

Head Bands

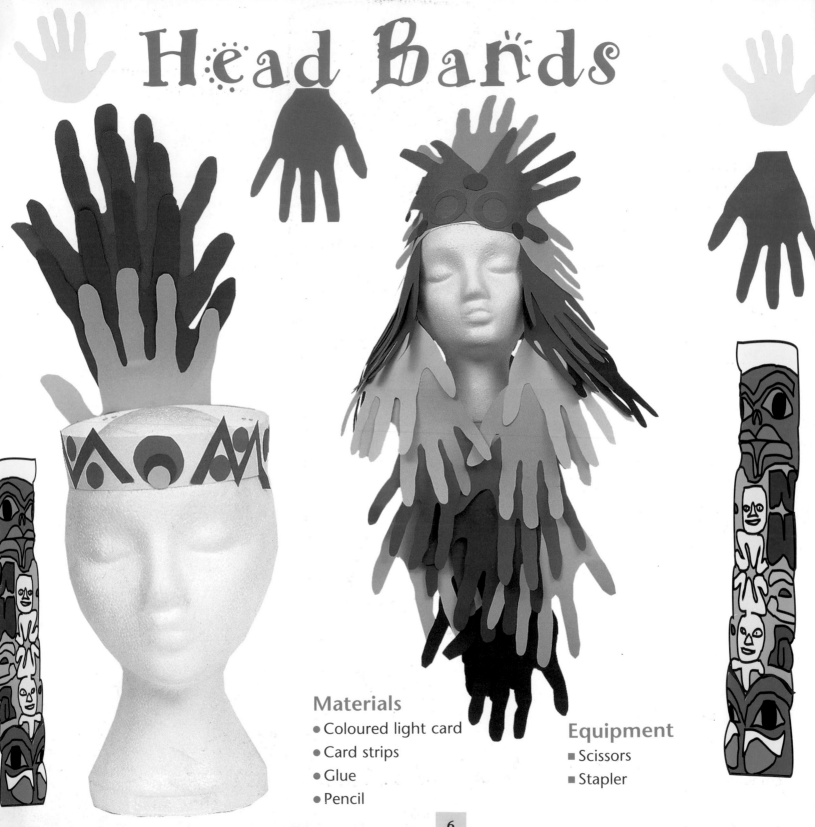

Materials
- Coloured light card
- Card strips
- Glue
- Pencil

Equipment
- Scissors
- Stapler

6

Suggested Themes

Chief headdress
Squaw headdress
Brave headdress

Trouble Shooter

Don't move your hand when drawing around it.

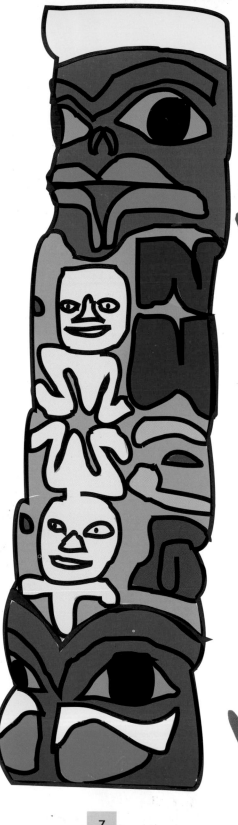

Preparation

Cut card strips 54cm long and 4cm wide.

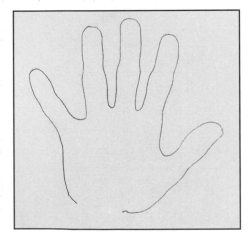

1 Spread your hand out on a piece of coloured card and draw around it with a pencil.

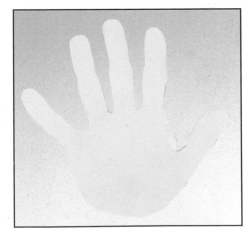

2 Cut the hand out very carefully with a scissors.

3 Repeat this many times with lots of different colours.

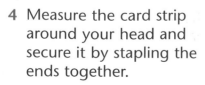

4 Measure the card strip around your head and secure it by stapling the ends together.

5 Glue the hands around the band, arranging them to form the headdress.

6 Add any extra decoration you choose.

Bats

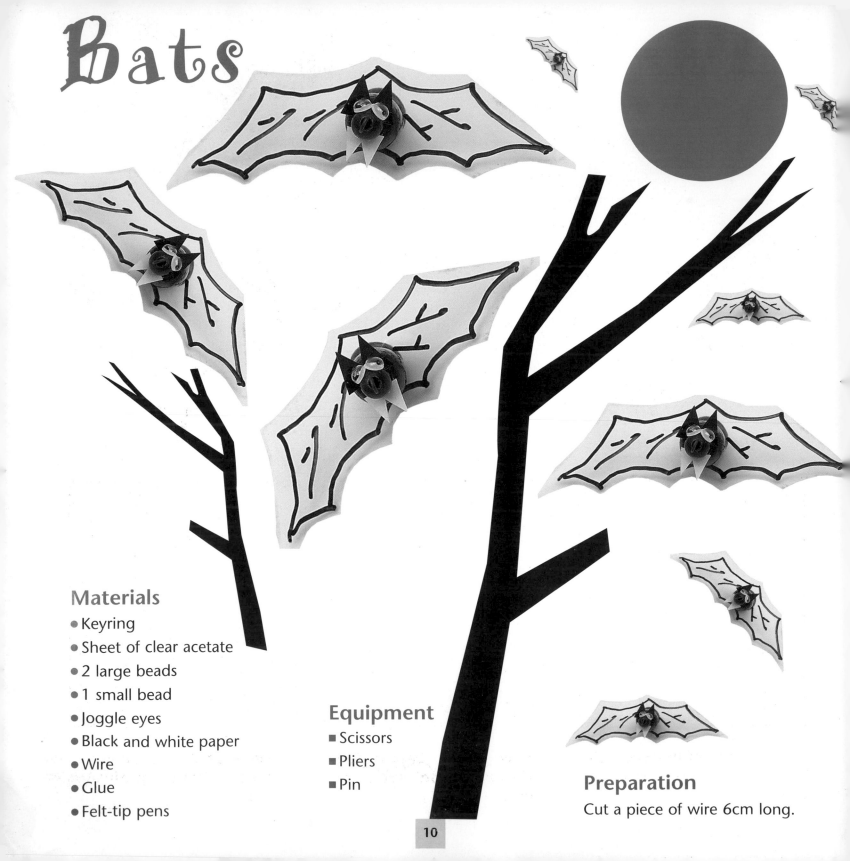

Materials
- Keyring
- Sheet of clear acetate
- 2 large beads
- 1 small bead
- Joggle eyes
- Black and white paper
- Wire
- Glue
- Felt-tip pens

Equipment
- Scissors
- Pliers
- Pin

Preparation
Cut a piece of wire 6cm long.

10

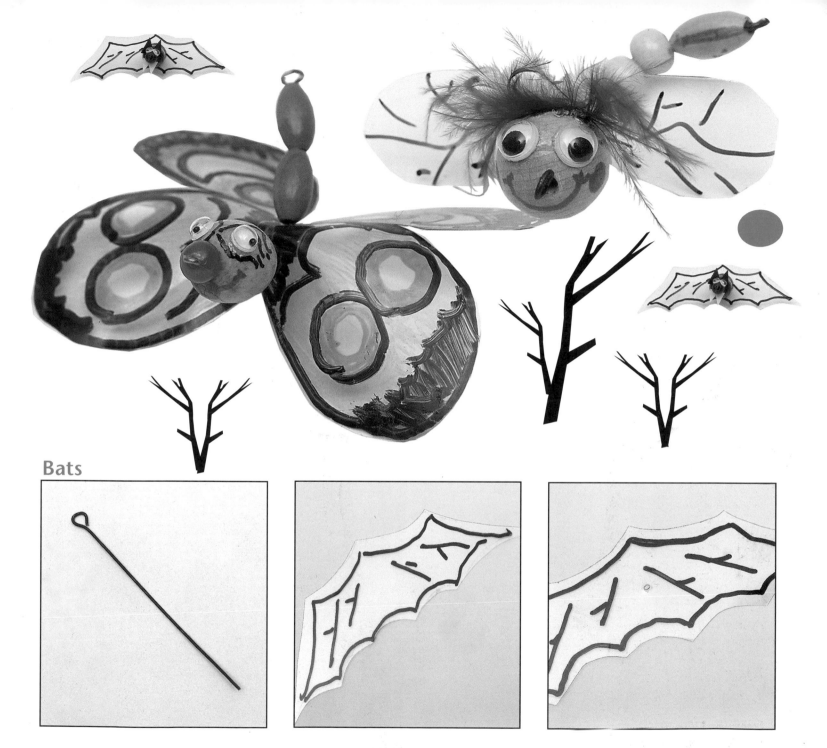

Bats

1 At one end of the wire make a loop with the pliers.

2 Draw a pair of bat wings on clear acetate and cut them out.

3 Pierce a hole through the centre of the wings with a pin.

4 Thread one small bead, one big bead, the wings and another big bead onto the wire.

5 With a pliers, turn a loop at the end of the wire.

6 Cut out a pair of ears and big white fangs.

Trouble Shooter

Put the glue onto the head, then place the joggle eyes into the glue on the head.

7 Glue them in place behind the small bead.

8 Glue joggle eyes in place.

9 Using the pliers, attach the keyring to the end loop.

13

Birds

Materials
- Cotton balls
- Air-drying modelling material
- Pipe cleaners
- PVA glue
- Powder paint – assorted colours

Equipment
- Mixing cups
- Wooden skewers

Preparation
With a skewer, mix the powder paint with PVA glue until it is creamy. Then with your hands, mix it into the modelling material, kneading it until it is all one colour.

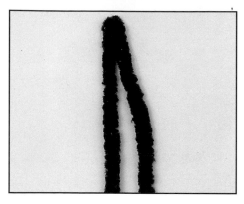

1 Bend a pipe cleaner in half.

2 Glue it into the centre of the cotton ball.

3 Take a piece of modelling material about the size of a small egg.

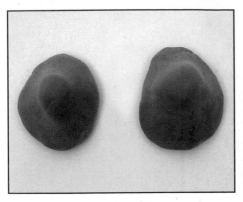

4 Divide it in two and form into cones.

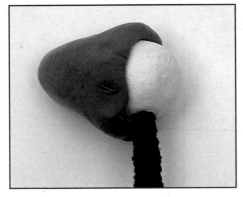

5 Place one cone over half the cotton ball.

6 Repeat on the other side. Seal the cones together, to make the body of the bird.

7 Make two eyes from small balls of modelling material. Attach them to the head.

8 Make the beak and attach it to the head.

9 Make two wings and attach them. Tease out the back end to make a tail.

Trouble Shooter

Make all the sections first and then stick them together. Air-drying modelling material sticks to itself as soon as it touches.

Teddy Bears' Picnic

Suggested Themes

Your family on holiday
A party
A scene from a story
An adventure in space or under
   the sea

Materials

- Wax crayons
- Cartridge paper
- Ink: black, blue and/or
   other colours
   or
- Dye

Equipment

- Soft brush
- Container for water
- Newspaper

Preparation

Cover the work surface with
newspaper.

Trouble Shooter

If the ink wash or dye is
too thick it will stick to
the crayon. If this
happens, wipe it off with
a damp tissue and add
more water to the mix.

Method

Draw your picture with crayon,
without filling in the
background. Apply the crayon
very thickly. Use light, bright
colours that will stand out
against a dull background. Put
lots of interesting things in
your picture. Thin the ink with
water. Using a soft brush, paint
all over the page. The crayon
work will resist the ink wash
and show through, while the
background is coloured by the
wash. You can use several
different colours of ink wash if
you wish.

1 Choose an interesting theme. Draw in brightly coloured crayon. Don't fill in the sky or the ground.

2 Select a colour or colours of ink that you think will look well with the crayoned picture. Mix a small amount with some water (about half and half) and paint all over the picture. The crayon will resist the water in the ink.

Funny Faces

Materials
- Modelling Clay: 1 kilo or less
- Acrylic paint

Equipment
- Board
- Modelling tools
  or
- Substitutes e.g. wooden skewer and lollipop stick
- Paint brushes
- Container for water
- Tissue to wipe brushes
- Newspaper

Preparation
Put a layer of newspaper on the work surface.
Lay the board for working on the newspaper.

Method
Follow the step-by-step method, pages 22–23, adapting it to the sort of funny face you want to make.

Trouble Shooter

Make sure the nose and ears and all the other features and additions are all well stuck on and rubbed in or they will fall off as the clay dries. Let your first layer of paint dry thoroughly before you add the details.

21

1 Divide your lump of clay into two pieces.

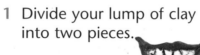

2 Make one piece into an egg shape or a ball.

6 Press the eyes and mouth firmly in place and smooth the clay well in.

7 Make sure the main features are well attached, then add some eyebrows and ears.

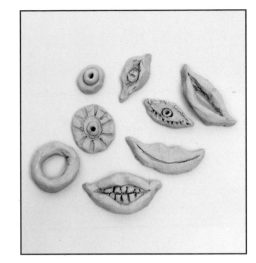

3 Press the egg or ball down on the board so that the back is flat.

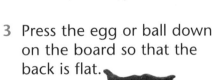

4 Using some of the other piece of clay, make some eyes and mouths. Try them out on your face and decide which you like.

5 Make a nose. You could make it like an ice-cream cone or a ball. Press it firmly in place and rub in the sides.

8 Put on some hair, beard and moustache if wanted; also a hat or headdress or any other detail.

9 When the clay face is dry, paint it in two stages. First paint the skin, hair and any big areas.

10 Then, when the paint is dry, paint the details – eyes, mouth, ears.

Animals

WOOLLY SMOOTH PRICKLY ANIMALS

PAINT WHAT THEY FEEL LIKE

Materials

- Paper: white or coloured
- Paint
- Pencil

Equipment

- Brushes: thick and thin
- Container of water
- Newspaper
- Tissue for wiping brushes

Preparation

Spread the newspapers on the work surface so that it doesn't matter if you paint over the edge of the picture.
Place the water, paint and brushes within easy reach.

Method

Follow the step-by-step pictures – pages 25–26. Use different brush strokes to make the paint look as if it was woolly, smooth or spiky.

WOOLLY

SPIKY

SMOOTH

Woolly Sheep

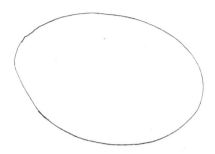 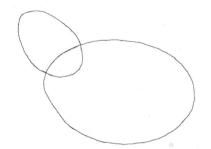 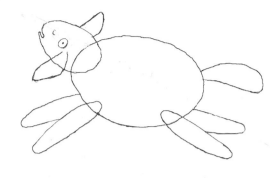

1 Draw an egg shape for the body, using either a light-colour paint with your thin paintbrush or use a pencil.

2 Draw a smaller egg shape for the head. Draw it so that part of the egg shape comes a bit inside the body egg shape.

3 Add eyes, ears, legs and a tail. Put an extra bit under the sheep's nose if you want its mouth open.

4 Put plenty of black paint on your brush. Keep the paint as dry as possible when you are painting in the head, ears and legs.

5 To make the sheep look as if it would feel woolly if you touched it, put lots of white paint on your brush and make it go round and round as you paint. To make the 'wool' seem thick, add a tiny little bit of black here and there as you swirl the paint around. Don't forget to paint some wool on top of the sheep's head.

6 Add some flowers and grass to your picture and any other detail you like. Make the grass seem spiky by using lots of short straight strokes together.

MORE SHEEP

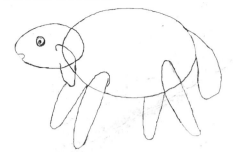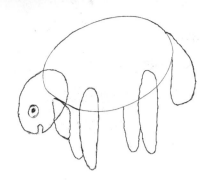

You can put the sheep's head, legs, ears and tail at different angles.
Head down when eating grass. Head up and legs bent when gambolling.

PRICKLY HEDGEHOG

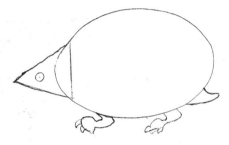

1 Start the hedgehog the same way as the sheep by drawing an egg shape for the body. Add a triangle for the head and short legs and tail.

2 Paint the hedgehog dark brown all over, keeping the paint as dry as possible. Mark in the eyes, nose and claws in black.

3 Make the hedgehog's prickles by painting long and short strokes of grey going backwards all over its body.

SMOOTH TORTOISE

1 Draw an egg shape for the body. Draw a small egg shape on a neck for the head and short thick legs and a tail.

2 Paint the head, legs and tail grey-green or whatever other colour you choose. Starting at the top, in the middle, outline the pattern on the tortoise's shell in a dark colour.

3 Fill in the pattern with a light and medium colour, keeping the light colour in the centre of each piece of the pattern. Add an eye and claws.

THEN ADD THE WOOLLY BITS

Trouble Shooter

Keep the paint dry, especially the main colour of the animal's body. If you are painting a flock of sheep, paint sheep at the back first.

Aquarium

Materials

- Polystyrene plates
- Pencil
- Tissue box
- Chalk
  or
- Water-based crayons
- Coloured paper

Equipment

- Ruler
- Scissors
- Sticky tape
- Needle
- Thread

Trouble Shooter

Before deciding what sort of crayon or chalk to use to colour your fish and seaweed, try them out on a piece of polystyrene as not all colours work well on it.

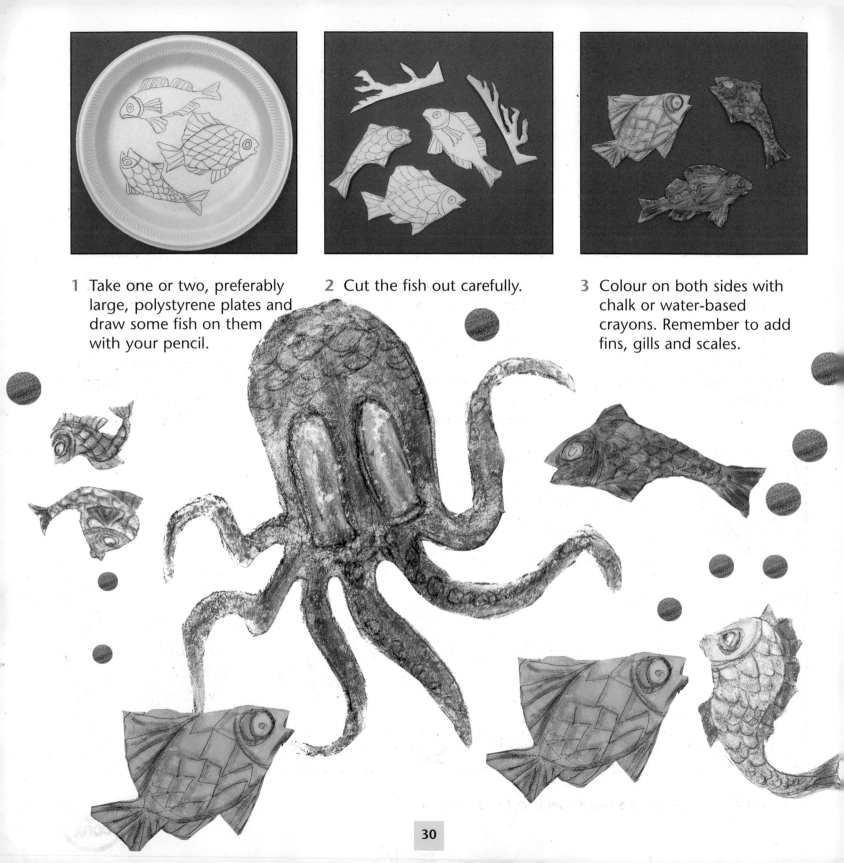

1 Take one or two, preferably large, polystyrene plates and draw some fish on them with your pencil.

2 Cut the fish out carefully.

3 Colour on both sides with chalk or water-based crayons. Remember to add fins, gills and scales.

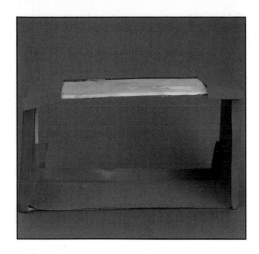  

4 Cut large windows in opposite sides of the tissue box. Cover the sides and bottom of the box with coloured paper. Leave the top until you have attached the fish.

5 With the needle, thread through the top of each fish so that it hangs evenly. Use about 30cm of thread. Decide how high you want to hang each fish and attach the thread to the top of the box with sticky tape.

6 From the remaining bits of polystyrene, cut some seaweed shapes and anything else, such as an octopus, that you would like to put in. Colour them and attach them inside the aquarium with sticky tape.

7 Cover the top of the aquarium with coloured paper.

Notes for Teachers

Pages 4–5 LEAVES
- **Concept** – awareness of shape, pattern and colour
- **Strand skill** – making colour images
- **Aim** – 'developing sensitivity to qualities of line, shape and colour in the natural environment'

Pages 6–9 HEAD BANDS
- **Concept** – awareness of shape, colour and tone
- **Strand skill** – making constructions
- **Aim** – 'using shape, colour and tone to create unity and emphasis'

Pages 10–13 BATS
- **Concept** – awareness of form
- **Strand skill** – making constructions
- **Aim** – 'becoming aware of the three-dimensional nature of form in the visual environment'

Pages 14–17 BIRDS
- **Concept** – awareness of form
- **Strand skill** – developing form
- **Aim** – 'using the medium expressively and exploring the relationship between the parts and the whole form'

Pages 18–19 TEDDY BEARS' PICNIC
- **Concept** – awareness of colour and tone
- **Strand skill** – using colour
- **Aim** – 'exploring the expressive and descriptive effects of a variety of colour media'

Pages 20–23 FUNNY FACES
- **Concept** – awareness of form
- **Strand skill** – developing form in clay
- **Aim** – 'experiencing the ideal medium for learning about form'

Pages 24–27 ANIMALS
- **Concept** – awareness of texture
- **Strand skill** – painting
- **Aim** – 'exploring the relationship between how things feel and how they look'

Pages 28–31 AQUARIUM
- **Concept** – awareness of space
- **Strand skill** – making constructions
- **Aim** – 'investigating the properties and characteristics of materials in making structures'